STEVEN BUTLER 🐾

DOG DIARIES

HAPPY OWLIDAYS!

🐾 AND JAMES PATTERSON

Illustrated by
RICHARD WATSON

1 3 5 7 9 10 8 6 4 2

Young Arrow
20 Vauxhall Bridge Road
London SW1V 2SA

Young Arrow is part of the Penguin Random House group of companies
whose addresses can be found at global.penguinrandomhouse.com

Penguin
Random House
UK

Copyright © James Patterson 2018
Illustrations by Richard Watson

James Patterson has asserted his right to be identified as the author of this
Work in accordance with the Copyright, Designs and Patents Act 1988

First published by Young Arrow in 2018

www.penguin.co.uk

A CIP catalogue record for this book is available from the British Library

ISBN 9781529119589

Printed and bound in Great Britain by
Clays Ltd, Elcograf S.p.A.

Penguin Random House is committed to a sustainable future for our
business, our readers and our planet. This book is made from Forest
Stewardship Council® certified paper.

For Wilson, Lyra and Louis

– S.B.

HELLO, MY FURLESS FRIEND!!
Oh boy, oh boy, OH BOY…you opened my new book!

I tell ya, I couldn't be more excited to know you're holding *HAPPY HOWLIDAYS!* in your five fingery digits, and we're about to go on a festive adventure together. Humans are my favorite…you're THE GREATEST, and I can feel a yip-yappy Happy Dance coming on. This is a bark-tastic moment! It's WAGGY-TAIL-ICIOUS!!

WOAH…hang on a second…I'm getting way ahead of myself.

What if you've not read any of my PAW-SOME stories before?

Could that be possible?

Well, if you haven't, I'd say you're in desperate need of some serious pooch-ification.

Now, I know what you're probably thinking. You'll be sat there right now, scratching your head in that way that humans do even when they haven't got fleas, wondering to yourself…*Pooch-ification? What's that?*

Don't you worry, my person-pal, I'll explain all of it. Y'see, my book is practically a manual of muttness. It's a canine crash course! SLOBBER SCHOOL!

If you read this dog diary, you'll be living a happier, bouncier, barking-at-raccoons-in-the-backyard-ier life in no time. I PROMISE!

But there are definitely a few things you should know before we dive in, snout-first.

First of all, I'M JUNIOR...HELLO!

Ha! I love saying that!

Dogs don't usually bother with hellos. We normally just take a quick sniff of each other's butts, but I learned early on that humans aren't so into that…HA HA!

The other thing I need to tell you about is…well…ummm…I didn't want to start things off like this, my furless friend, but there's no way around it. For me to begin this story properly…like PROPERLY-PROPERLY…you need to hear about what I've been up to, and it includes one of the ugliest words in the Doglish language…it's a HORRIBLE word…DISGUSTING!! Even the bravest of hounds have run howling for the hills at the sound of it!

Brace yourself, before you turn the page.

Steady those nerves.

Breathe in...breathe out...then hide yourself in the laundry pile or under your bed.

Are you ready? Okay...

UGH! It's one of the worst words ever, and I heard it WAY TOO MANY TIMES this summer.

Yep…if you've not read Book One in my totally lick-a-rific series, you missed out on hearing all about how I had to endure the nightmarish…the no-tummy-rubs-or-treats-ish…PERFECT POOCH OBEDIENCE SCHOOL FOR DOGS.

It was awful, my person-pal! There were moments back in those classes at the Hills Village dog park when I felt sure I was a goner. I thought my brain was going to melt into a big blob of Meaty-Giblet-Jumble-Chum and ooze out of my ears, IT WAS SOOOOOO BORING!!

Imagine it! A poor pooch like me being stuck with Iona Stricker and her pampered poodle, having to roll over, sit down, and play dead, when I should have been chasing raccoons and sniffing around the jungle gym with my bestest mutt-mates.

"WHAT A WAY TO SPEND YOUR SUMMER, JUNIOR!" I hear you say…

But don't you fret, my furless friend. You didn't think I gave in to old Stricty-Pants Stricker, did you?

NEVER!!

I sure showed her. I don't want to give too much away, but it was me who walked away from the annual DEBONAIR DANDY-DOG SHOW with a year's supply of dog food and not Stricker's prim and proper princess-poodle Duchess. But I'm not gonna tell you how…

Ha ha! I wish you could have been there, my friend, it was TERRIFIC! But I couldn't have done any of it without the help of my best-best-BESTEST pet human, Ruff Catch-A-Doggy-Bone.

Just look at that face. I swear, I adore all you BRILLIANT humans, but there's nobody in the whole world that makes me wag my tail and perform a Happy Dance like Ruff. He's the greatest pet a dog like me could wish for.

RAFE KHATCHADORIAN

Ruff Catch-A-Doggy-Bone

×

Anyway...where was I? Ah yes, I'd say that's about enough snuffling down memory lane for now. We're already on page 10 and there's SO much more I need to tell you about.

You see, crazy things have been happening around Hills Village. REALLY WEIRD THINGS!!

I mean it, my person-pal. You won't believe your ears when I tell you what's been going on.

Are you now ready to dive in, snout-first?

Okay...don't forget to bring some treats and maybe a chew toy in case you need a few breaks along the way. I promise to tell you all the good bits and I won't leave any of it out.

Here we go!!

Tuesday

Now, I don't know what you and your human families like to get up to in your home towns, but here in Hills Village things get real strange toward the end of the year when everything gets colder.

I'd heard about all this weird stuff before, but with all the chaos and business of obedience classes (YUCK!!) over the summer, it had completely slipped my mutt-mind.

It wasn't until a few days ago when I was minding my own business, chewing a Twisty-Chum-Chomper-Stick that I'd hidden in the Picture Box Room, that I heard Mom-Lady talking to Grandmoo on the chatty-ear-stick...

We've got LOTS of planning to do. It's nearly the HOLIDAY SEASON!

The Howliday Season!

It couldn't be true, could it? The fabled human howlidays of myth and legend?!

Oooh, I should probably explain myself…

A quick history…

Let's go back to my days at the Hills Village Dog Shelter, or, as us mutts like to call it, "POOCH PRISON": Me and my four-legged friends were stuck in a cage right next to Old Mama Mange. She was very, very, very, very, very old and had been behind bars for as long as anyone could remember—practically a squillion centuries when you think about it in dog years.

Anyway…late at night, when the warden had nodded off in front of the picture box in his office, Old Mama Mange would hobble up to the bars and tell us the most amazing stories from her life before she ended up in the slobbering slammer...the canine clink!

All her stories were most excellent, but there was one she'd gabble on about more than any other…

17

And the humans have a whole season of **HOWLIDAYS**, filled with fangs givings and a great big ho-ho-ho-er named **SAINT LICK!**

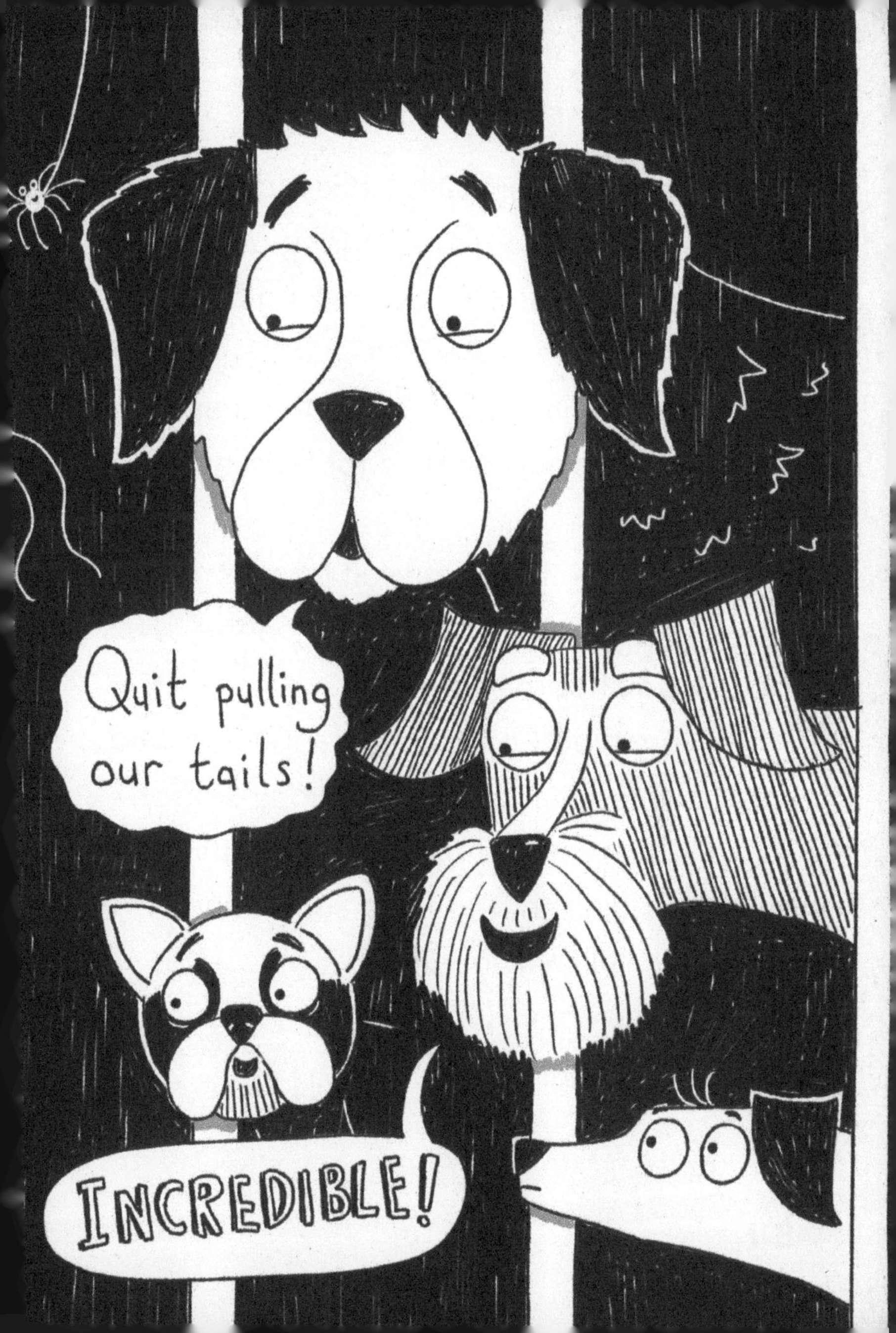
Quit pulling our tails!
INCREDIBLE!

None of us ever really believed her, but now there I was, overhearing my own Catch-A-Doggy-Bone pack talking about THE HOWLIDAY SEASON!

Have you ever heard of anything as exciting as a whole season for howling?!?! Well, I hadn't!

I could barely stop myself from leaping into a Happy Dance right there on the Picture Box Room rug!

If everything Old Mama Mange had said was completely true, the Howliday Season was the biggest and best of all the human howlidays, and that's saying something. The people of Hills Village LOVE 'EM! They have so many, it's hard to count on all four paws.

I'm not even joking, my furless friend! I got a good look at Mom-Lady's calendar on the Food Room wall once and it was practically stuffed with howlidays of all sorts.

Don't believe me? I'll tell you...

The year starts with NEW EARS DAY.

Then there's MARTIN LUTHER KING CHARLES CAVALIER'S BIRTHDAY. I'm not sure who he was, but he seems like one important spaniel.

There's GEORGE WASHY-TONGUE'S
BIRTHDAY...the lickiest President there
ever was.

In the summer there's INKY-PEN-DANCE
DAY! This is a real big party. It's a special
howliday for scribbling all over the walls,
then celebrating with enormous flashy sky-
bangers! Us pooches are terrified of them,
but the humans of Hills Village can't get
enough.

AND THEN…

TA-DAA! We get to the best of them all! THE HOWLIDAY SEASON!!

The biggest and most bark-tastic part of the year…

Old Mama Mange told us so many stories about Fangs Giving and Crisp-Mouth Day and it all sounds SO much fun. A howliday where you get brand-new teeth, followed by one filled with nothing but stuffing your mouth with CANINE CRISPY CRACKERS?!?!

BLISS!!!

Wednesday

I can barely contain my excitement, my person-pal. It's all coming true!

Ever since I heard Mom-Lady mention the Howliday Season on the chatty-ear-stick, I've been keeping my pooch-peepers on high alert for clues.

And guess what? THERE ARE CLUES EVERYWHERE! Just look at the backyard! It's all changing and I can definitely tell that my first-ever winter outside of the Hills Village Dog Shelter is on its way.

Come on, I'll show you...

This all HAS to be something to do with the Howliday Season, I'm sure of it!

It's all very paw-some! I have no idea why the trees have gone bald and left their leaves on the ground. Go figure! Maybe they're getting real old? Maybe they've just been careless, or maybe they left them as a gift to all the people and pooches out there?

I mean it!! I can't think of anything nicer!

If you've never kicked about through a pile of crisp leaves before, you are definitely in need of a little more pooch-ification, my furless friend. It's one of my favorite poochish pastimes!

So far it's definitely been the best part of the howlidays...

Ooooooh, speaking of the best part of the howlidays...the next special event of the season is happening tomorrow, and I'm feeling giddy about this one!

With the backyard all crunch-ified and whispers of excitement in the air, I've been listening to every conversation that happens at mealtime and I'm taking note of anything that sounds remotely howliday-ish. I'm learning SO MUCH about all the strange things people like to celebrate at this time of year, and most of it is completely BONKERS!

This next special day is the first BIG ONE of the season.

YOU GUESSED IT…

FANGS GIVING!!

Everyone in the Catch-A-Doggy-Bone pack seem to be super excited about it…

including me!

Imagine a special day all about giving other people a new set of chompers. I couldn't invent a more poochish celebration if I tried!

I personally couldn't be prouder that Ruff, Jawjaw, Mom-Lady, and even Grandmoo are finally going to get their properly proper canine teeth and become more poochish than ever! They'll be chomping their way through all sorts of things in no time! If they're lucky, I might even show them the best chair leg to chew on in the Food Room, or what kind of tasty stinky socks are easiest to shred, ha ha!

9 a.m.

Oh boy, oh boy, OH BOY! I can tell that Fangs Giving is going to be just TERRIFIC! How could it not be?

Mom-Lady says we're going to feast on TURKEY tomorrow, and she needs to go and pick it up, ready for the family feast!

I definitely know what turkey is! There's no mystery there…no sirree. I know EXACTLY what it is. After all, I've tried it lots of times!

Turkeys are lumpy, squidgy, smooshy blob-creatures who are kinda pinky/grayish in color and they live in little metal Meaty-Giblet-Jumble-Chum cans.

Ha! Told you I knew!!

It's the strangest of animals to look at, all gloopy dollops. It doesn't do much, but it really, really loves sitting in food bowls and being eaten, which is very lucky because it's also DEEEEEEEELICIOUS!!

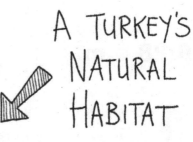

A TURKEY'S NATURAL HABITAT

MEATY- GIBLET -JUMBLE- CHUM

TURKEY FLAVOR

9:28 a.m.

And we're off, my person-pal. Mom-Lady and I are in the moving people-box on wheels and we're heading to the turkey farm to pick up our very own EXTRA-LARGE turkey!

Whoever heard of a turkey farm?!? I've never seen one before, but I'm willing to bet it looks a lot like this...

11:33 a.m.

Errrm…

We've just arrived back at the kennel and Mom-Lady carried something huge out of the back of the moving people-box on wheels. I sat in the front seat the whole time but didn't see our extra-large turkey when she collected it at the farm store and put it in the trunk. Only, just now,

I caught a glimpse of it as Mom-Lady went into the Food Room...and it's MASSIVE!!

Extra-large cans of food aren't usually *that* much bigger than the regular kind—this thing was the size of all Ruff's Sleep Room pillows piled together! It was inside a huge shopping bag, so I didn't get a good look, but OH BOY are we going to be feasting tomorrow!

12 p.m.

Aaaagh! This is so frustrating, my person-pal! All I want to do is get a peek at the enormous can of turkey, but Mom-Lady has banned me, Ruff, and Jawjaw from going into the Food Room. She says…

1 p.m.

Ruff and Jawjaw have been set the task of decorating the Picture Box Room, so I've tagged along to watch.

It's so funny to us dogs how humans hang stuff up on walls to celebrate an occasion. You can be super strange sometimes, HA HA! I just don't get what it's for…

I remember feeling SO confused back in the springtime when we had a party for Grandmoo—because she'd turned another year older, I think. I just couldn't understand why Mom-Lady was so worried about hanging up long ropes of little flaggy things and blowing up colorful blobs filled with her breath, when there were far more important things to pay attention to...like the table FILLED with food or barking through the front door every time another guest arrived.

Anyway...Ruff is now hanging twisty loops of yellowy/leafy twigs on the wall, and Jawjaw has been arranging little round orange things on the window ledge. At first I thought they were balls for playing fetch with and snatched one when Jawjaw wasn't looking, but the whole thing turned out to be some sort of vegetable and went crunch in my mouth when I least expected it. Loads of stringy seeds and bits of squidgy goop exploded everywhere!

Why would humans want to decorate their kennels with exploding VEGETABLES???

NOTE TO SELF:

Keep away from the little orange decorations—they taste like poop and healthy stuff. BLEEEUUUGH!!!!

47

2:17 p.m.

There are wonderful, nose-tickling smells wafting down the hallway from the Food Room and I'm trying to do anything I can to not think about the giant can of dog food we're all going to be enjoying for Fangs Giving tomorrow. Be still, my houndy heart!!

3:21 p.m.

This is unbearable! Whatever Mom-Lady is cooking up on the other side of the Food Room door smells so delicious I've lost control of my paws. My feet keep hopping and twitching about with pure excitement!!

4:45 p.m.

I'm not going to make it to Fangs Giving at this rate, my furless friend. All the whiff-tastic smells are making my stomach growl louder than a bear with a bellyache!

4:57 p.m.

I…I…I can't concentrate…I can't relax…I can't stop myself from drooling at the thought of all that turkey…

Mom-Lady put my regular food bowl in the hall while she's cooking, but I can't even look at my normal food anymore. It's just so UN-TURKEY-ISH! I'm going to drool myself to death…

5:04 p.m.

Any minute now...I...I...I can feel my life slipping away...*cough*... GOODBYE, CRUEL WORLD! I can't go on a minute longer without that turkey tastiness... *splutter*...just need a...*whimper*...turkey treat...or...seven...

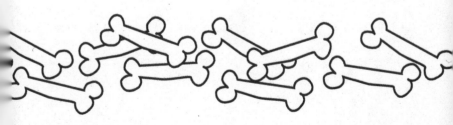

5:12 p.m.

DEAD!

5:36 p.m.

STILL DEAD!

5:46 p.m.

EVEN MORE DEAD!

5:51 p.m.

SO DEAD, I
COULDN'T GET
ANY DEADER!!

53

6 p.m.

Okay, okay, okay...I'm not dead! I may have overreacted a little, but that was a close one, I'm telling ya!

I finally managed to distract myself from all the yumma-lumptious smells by sneaking into Jawjaw's room and stealing one of the creepy little plastic humans she keeps on the shelf above her bed.

Hey! Don't judge me, alright? These are desperate times, and only one of the *forbidden* chew toys was enough to take my mind off things. Who could blame me at a time like this, anyway?

I'm never supposed to go in Jawjaw's Sleep Room. She gets super grumpalicious if I ever sneak inside. Yep! It's strictly out of bounds...so, of course, the things inside her room taste far more interesting than anything else around the kennel.

I've stashed it in Ruff's laundry pile for now, though. He's been calling me from the Picture Box Room and I don't want to be found out. I'll go see what he wants...

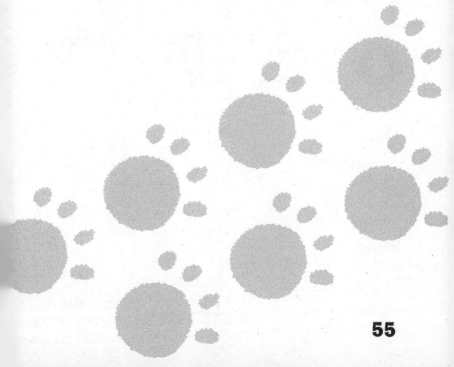

7:33 p.m.

Check, check… This is roving reporter Junior Catch-A-Doggy-Bone, coming to you live from the comfy squishy thing.

BREAKING NEWS

Ha ha! Just joking with you! I've always wanted to say that after seeing it on the picture box.

But…guess what? Ruff and I snuggled in to watch a program all about Fangs Giving and I'm learning heaps about it. I mean…my understanding of the Peoplish language is a little crummy, but I think I've got the basics of the Fangs Giving story. Wanna hear?

Okay…settle down, get all comfy and listen to this…

THE STORY OF FANGS GIVING

Long, long ago, when the world was practically a puppy and Meaty-Giblet-Jumble-Chum hadn't even been invented yet, a pack of Pilgrim Pooches and their pet humans swam all the way to Hills Village from the other side of the planet. WHOOO-WEEEE, that's a long way!

They bravely traveled into the unknown, looking for a life filled with mountains of treats, super-tickly tummy-rubs, and a comfortable place to poop, but when they arrived, they discovered a pack of majestic native Hills Village-ians instead.

At first, the Hills Village-ians and their hunting hounds were very wary of the Pilgrim Pooches and their pet humans, but before long they all got together for a doggy-licious dinner party—they ate a lot, danced a lot, and ever since then, on the fourth Thursday of November, families get together to celebrate and give fangs to those who need 'em. That explains the name of the howliday!

THE END...

There! I definitely missed a few facts along the way, but I'm pretty sure I got most of the story right. It all makes so much more sense now…sort of…

10:30 p.m.

I can't sleep, my furless friend. Everyone headed off to their Sleep Rooms early, ready for a big day of celebrating tomorrow, but I just can't get the thought of all that marvelous meat out of my brain.

I've tried everything I can, but nothing works! Putting my head under Ruff's pillow. Lying on my back with my paws in the air. Counting sheep in my head. That last one is something Old Mama Mange told me to try when we were having a bad night back in pooch prison. But before I'd even realized it, the sheep had transformed themselves into cans of delicious turkey and were taunting me with their tastiness.

11:08 p.m.

There's nothing for it, my person-pal. If I stand any chance of getting to sleep tonight, I'm going to have to go and take just the tiniest of peeks at what Mom-Lady has prepared in the Food Room.

Now, I know what you're thinking. You're reading this and saying, "No! Junior, you're going to get into so much trouble! You'll never be able to resist all that belly-bungling food!" and you'd be right... normally.

But...I have a cunning plan. Just to make sure I'm not tempted to snack on anything and get myself into hot water, I'm bringing along Jawjaw's creepy little plastic human I stashed in the laundry pile earlier. That way, if I have any sudden urges to gobble up what Mom-Lady's cooked, I can chew on the plastic toy instead. IT'S FOOLPROOF!

11:45 p.m.

Psssst! Are you there? Oh good...it's so dark in the hallway.

Okay, I'm just going to sneak into the Food Room, take a quick look around, and I'll be out of there and back on the bed in a jiffy. No harm done, right?

Here I go...

66

Midnight

HOLD EVERYTHING!!! I know it's late, my furless friend, but I've just gotta tell you about what I saw. You wouldn't believe your person-peepers.

I nudged the Food Room door open and was instantly hit by a dizzying mix of fantastic aromas and delicious whiffs. One of the little lights above the counter had been left on, so I got a good view of everything, and...well...I'm not afraid to admit it brought a tear to this mutt's eye.

The table had been decorated with fancy cloths and decked out with flowers and candles and more of those little exploding orange vegetables. Mom-Lady had been baking all day and there were biscuits and rolls piled up under a glass dome.

The kitchen counter was lined with bowls and dishes of tasty-smelling foods and sauces, waiting to be cooked and feasted upon for tomorrow's Fangs Giving dinner, and...

I looked up...

I looked down...

I sniffed in every corner of the room...

Where was the enormous can of turkey? It had to be here someplace.

I snuffled about the room for a few minutes, trying to figure out where it could be. The turkey can wasn't on the table, and it wasn't lined up on the counter ready to be cooked.

Just then a thought flashed across my barky-brain and I gasped. There was only one place Mom-Lady kept the meaty food before she cooked it in the hot fire box for dinner...

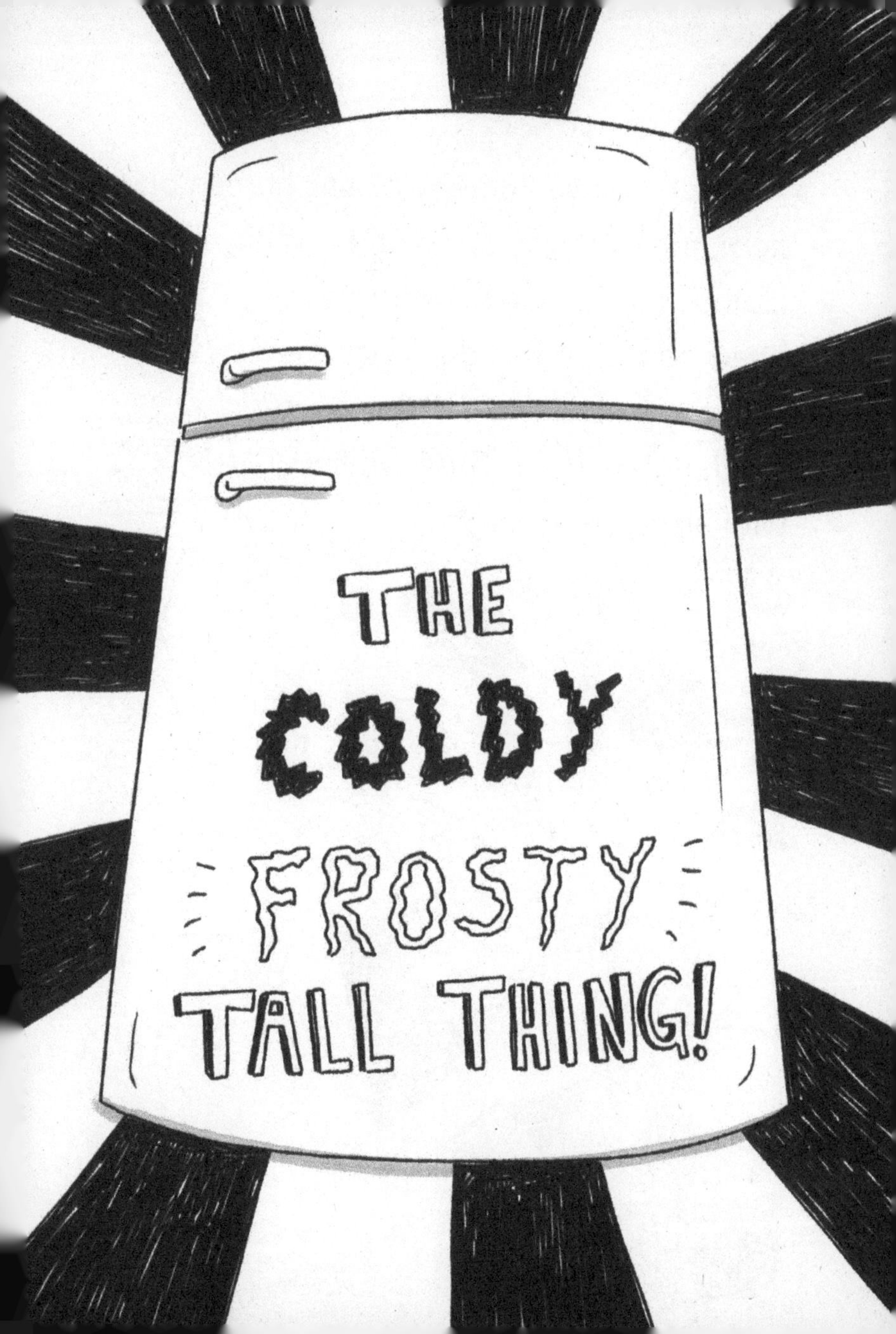

THE
COLDY
FROSTY
TALL THING!

I put Jawjaw's creepy plastic human on the floor, then grabbed one of the stinky wash cloths from its hook. Swinging my head from side to side, I managed to loop it through the coldy frosty tall thing's handle. Then I pulled with all my mutt-might.

At first the door didn't want to budge. I struggled and tugged but nothing moved.

I couldn't give up now! There was no way I was going to leave the Food Room without seeing the turkey for myself. With thoughts of the giant can of meat skipping across my mind, I gave it one last enormous yank and the coldy frosty tall thing burst open in a cloud of chilly fog.

For a second, the bright light from inside the tall box blinded me and I squinted my eyes against it. My fur prickled with a mixture of excitement and the icy air that swirled around my paws.

This was it: I was going to see the…

AAAAAAAAAGH!!

Suddenly my houndy heart leaped up into my throat as I saw what was sitting in the fridge.

There must be some mistake. Had Mom-Lady gone absolutely crazy?!

Instead of a neat tin can filled with squidgy blobby globs of turkey, she'd brought home some kind of giant headless BALDY BIRD!!

I scampered across the floor and darted under the table, expecting the ugly creature to attack at any moment.

Safely tucked behind the tablecloth, I tried to stop myself from panting with surprise and listened as hard as I could for signs that the great big baldy beast was preparing to pounce.

I waited…

    I waited…

        I waited…

            Nothing.

Sniffing the air, I peeked out from under the cloth and stared at the weird animal sitting in the open coldy frosty tall thing. I gave it a few test growls and even tried darting toward it and then running away very fast to see what it did.

The baldy bird didn't move.

I sniffed the air again and caught the scent of salty, fatty deliciousness. It was even better than the pong of Meaty-Giblet-Jumble-Chum!

Maybe this beast in the cold box wasn't a dog-eating terror from the land of nightmares.

I crept back toward it, preparing to dart away at a second's notice, but still the creature didn't move.

It just sat there like Lola after she's snaffled down a full bowl of Doggo-Drops.

Now I was close, I could see it was sitting in a big tray filled with sliced vegetables and green leafy stuff. Mom-

Lady had covered it in zingy-
smelling oil and sprinkled
salt and pepper all over it.
WOWZERS! This was one
pampered partridge...a glamorous
goose...A LUXURIOUS LUNCH!! Ha ha!

There was an opening in the baldy bird (I
think it was its mouth), and Mom-Lady had
put lots of sliced lemons and tufts of green
stuff in there. I guess the strange thing must
have been hungry.

Just then I couldn't help but feel a little
sorry for the salty and peppery baldy bird.
It certainly wasn't going to be able to join
in the fun of Fangs Giving after it went to
cook in the hot fire box tomorrow morning,
so I decided to give it a gift, just from me. It
is the Howliday Season, after all...

I grabbed Jawjaw's creepy little human and placed it in with the sliced lemons and tufty leaves. That way the baldy bird could have one last night of waggy-tail-icious snacking on one of the tastiest forbidden chew toys in the whole kennel. It was the least I could do...

12:24 a.m.

My work here is done, my person-pal. I've seen the festive baldy bird...I've spread a little howliday cheer...and I can feel a long, happy nap coming on.

See you tomorrow!

Thursday

6 a.m.

Wake up! Wake up! WAKE UP! Good morning, my furless friend. It's finally here!! Fangs Giving has arrived and I can't wait to celebrate with my new set of gnawy-gnashing fangs. I might try chewing through the tree in the backyard this afternoon! That'll surprise the raccoons!! Ha ha!

I'm just going to race about the kennel and wake everyone up the way they enjoy the most...with a good paw-poke right in the center of their forehead. Won't be a sec...

10 a.m.

No one has handed out the new teeth yet but Grandmoo's come over with cookies of the human and canine variety, and we're watching a huge parade on the picture box.

I swear I've never seen anything like it, but I couldn't be a happier hound...well... not until the feast. Ha! I can't wait to try great big baldy bird for the first time!!

2 p.m.

It's time!! We've all been summoned into the Food Room and we're preparing to sit down and feast together as the Catch-A-Doggy-Bone pack. Mom-Lady is even going to let me sit at the table with my own dog bowl filled with delicious dog-elicacies.

2:12 p.m.

Oh, you should see it, my person-pal! The table is all set...I'm not sure what all the foods are, but I listened real hard to Grandmoo, and as far as I can tell there's...

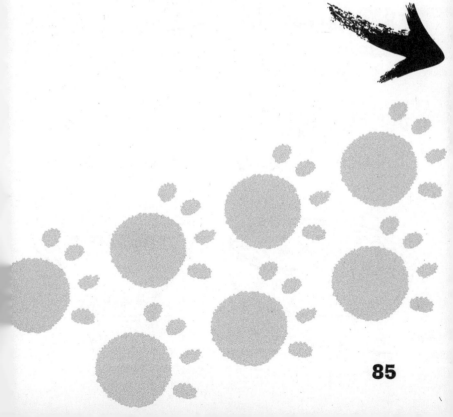

Swonk potatoes

Bumble-butt
squashed soup

Stuff

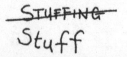

Groovy sauce

GREEN BEANS

Grim bean

CRANBERRY SAUCE

Crumb-bungle sauce

PECAN PIE

Peeking Pie

You name it, Mom-Lady has cooked it!
The only thing we're waiting for now
is the grand finale!! The great big roasted
baldy bird! It's going to be SPECTACULAR!!

87

2:16 p.m.

UH-OH! NO, NO, NO, NO, NO!!!
Mom-Lady has just pulled the bird
from the hot fire box and already I can smell
that something isn't right. My nose is super,
super, super stronger than my pet humans'
and I don't think they've noticed it yet, but
I definitely smell a plastic-ish, pong-whiffly
stink coming from the roast. Something tells
me I maybe shouldn't have put Jawjaw's

creepy little human inside the baldy bird before it was cooked.

I'll just keep quiet and hope no one notices…

4 p.m.

So much for no one noticing, my furless friend!!

One minute it was "HAPPY FANGS GIVING!" and the next it was…

5:26 p.m.

Oh, it's awful, my person-pal. I've never felt so rotten in my mutt-life.

Mom-Lady was furious when she found the melted creepy plastic human inside the turkey. I thought she was going to breathe flames and explode like one of the little orange vegetables!

To make matters worse, Mom-Lady blamed Jawjaw and sent her straight to her Sleep Room without any Fangs Giving snacks at all. I tried to explain that it was all my fault, I really did, but my pet humans are crummy at understanding Doglish and they just stared at me like I'd gone loop-the-loop Crazy with a capital C!!

I never intended to spoil the Fangs Giving feast and, even though I'm not one of Jawjaw's biggest fans, I didn't want to get her into trouble.

7:14 p.m.

Okay, my furless friend. I'm keeping a seriously low profile behind the comfy squishy thing in the Picture Box Room.

Mom-Lady ended up having to call in pizza, which put her in an even moodier mood after all the care she'd taken with the big baldy bird.

But...it's not all bad...I guess...

Ruff managed to convince his mom to order a triple chunky cheese and hot dog pizza with extra-crunchy crusts. OUR FAVORITE!!

Grandmoo complained all evening...

...and Mom-Lady refused to eat a single slice out of sheer grumpaliciousness, but Ruff and I actually had a pretty GREAT Fangs Giving feast all to ourselves.

I suppose you could almost say that by breaking the rules and sneaking into the Food Room when I wasn't supposed to… and putting the creepy little human (which I wasn't supposed to have) into the big baldy bird…and accidentally making the whole meal taste like burnt plastic…I actually improved the howliday, right?

OF COURSE I'M RIGHT!

Without my expert help, there would NEVER have been triple chunky cheese and hot dog pizza with extra-crunchy crusts at the Fangs Giving table…and everything's better with pizza. Ha ha!

Yep—after careful consideration, I'm pretty sure I actually saved the day.

I'm going to sleep well tonight, my person-pal. I just wish I could figure out when they're going to hand out the brand-new sets of fangs...

Saturday

10:20 a.m.

Hmmmm…I may have been a little wrong about saving Fangs Giving, my person-pal.

I mean…I definitely think I definitely saved it definitely…but Mom-Lady is still super mad about the feast being ruined

and I'm pretty certain Jawjaw is on to me.
In fact, I know she is!

She keeps scowling every time she sees
me…and…well…I wouldn't really mind—
after all, Jawjaw used to scowl at me long
before I spoiled the big baldy bird—but
now she keeps muttering two words under
her breath and they're the worst thing
a mutt like me could ever want to hear.
Especially from someone in his own pack.

It's true. Every time Jawjaw spots me
in the Picture Box Room or she walks past
Ruff's Sleep Room door and sees me curled
up on the bed, she scrunches up her face
and hisses…

Oh! They're the ugliest, scariest, most hateful words. My spine judders and I get a sickly swooshy feeling in my belly whenever someone says them out loud. It's left me feeling even guiltier than the time I buried Jawjaw's science project in the backyard and she got an F in class. That was a tail-between-my-legs kind of day, it really was, but this feels far worse...

Don't get me wrong—it's not the words Jawjaw said that are so horrible. It's what they mean and what they can lead to that scares us mutts. "Bad dog!" means no snacks. It means no tummy-rubs, or playing fetch in the dog park, or snuggles at bedtime, and...and...it can even mean a one-way ticket straight back to POOCH PRISON.

Ugh! I can hardly bring myself to say it!

I can't bear to think about Jawjaw seeing me as a B...a BA...a BAD...Oh, you know what I'm trying to say.

But triple chunky cheese and hot dog pizza with extra-crunchy crusts or no triple chunky cheese and hot dog pizza with extra-crunchy crusts, I can't let anything else go wrong this Howliday Season.

I've been hiding in the Rainy Poop Room a lot over the past few days and I've come up with a foolproof plan to make sure the Catch-A-Doggy-Bone pack have the best Crisp-Mouth Day EVER. I've decided that...

I, Junior Catch-A-Doggy-Bone, solemnly swear that, from now on, I'm going to be the biggest GOOD BOY Hills Village has ever seen. I will be even better behaved than a perfect pampered pedigree pooch princess. I will share all my Canine Crispy Crackers and make this the CRISPIEST season my pet humans have ever seen. I will howl the howliday songs with gusto, and I will do everything in my pooch power to make sure Ruff, Jawjaw, Grandmoo, and Mom-Lady are happier than a French bulldog with a Frisbee!
JUNIOR FOR PRESIDENT
VOTE JUNIOR
VOTE

11 a.m.

Phew! I feel much better, my furless friend. If I make sure to keep that in mind from here on out, I know I can save the festivities and make this a Howliday Season to remember. That way, no one will ever think I'm a BAD DOG again.

1:21 p.m.

Ooooh! Ooooh! Ooooh! That's enough worrying for now, my person-pal. You won't believe what I've just seen.

Mom-Lady needed to go to the grocery store across town and she said I could go too for a walk. YIP-YIP-YIPPEE!!

Now, I always love taking Mom-Lady for a walk. It's not as much fun as going with Ruff, obviously, but it definitely has its perks.

If I wait patiently outside and don't bark at the other shoppers as they rattle about with those strange shopping cages on wheels, she buys some slices of chicken from the deli counter and gives me a piece.

And that's not even the best part!

Mom-Lady really likes exercise and always takes the long route home, which means...DOGGY DRUMROLL, PLEASE!... we come back home via the Dandy Dog store!! It's one of my favorite places to visit in all of Hills Village, and I know that if I'm super good and I don't tug on the leash too much when we're walking, we can go in and have a good snuffle about.

I wish you could experience it, my person-pal. Behind that big green door is a pooch paradise, the likes of which you've never seen before. It's a dreamland for dogs! HOUND HEAVEN!!

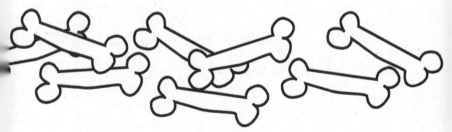

I get so excited when we go inside, I can't help but jump and yip about like a pup in a playground. It's a shouty-shuffle, but there's nothing I can do. You'd feel the same if you saw it, my furless friend, I just know you would. The Dandy Dog store is an entire shop filled with treats and snacks and toys and blankets and beds and balls and everything a dog could ever wish for.

But...it gets even better! You see, the best part of my walk with Mom-Lady wasn't just going inside my favorite shop, it was what I saw inside that wonderful place. Because today, on top of all the usual fantastic things to see and sniff and play with, the Dandy Dog store had been completely decorated!

My doggy eyes nearly rocketed out of my head with surprise. Everywhere I turned, there were twinkling lights and festive-looking red-and-white sticks hanging from the shelves. Jingly music was playing loudly and the shopkeeper was wearing a funny costume with pointy ears attached to his hat!

It was the most festiverous sight I'd ever laid my pooch-peepers on, I tell ya!

Mom-Lady gasped just as much as I did when she saw all the incredible decorations and hurried inside with me to have a look about.

I'd only had time to sniff the pile of braided rope toys when I spotted my pooch-pals Odin and Diego at the back of the store with their pet human and…

HA HA! Their pet had dressed them up in silly costumes just like the shopkeeper! Odin was wearing a knitted sweater with huge sprigs of holly on both sides, and Diego had on a little hat with a bell hanging off the end and little chihuahua-sized curly boots. It was HILARIOUS!

Even if nothing else happens for the rest of the year, seeing my pooch-pals all dressed up like that has to make this the BEST Howliday Season EVER!! HA HA!

2:17 p.m.

Oh no, my person-pal, I spoke too soon!! This is terrible!!

It turns out while I was distracted and laughing at my mutt-mates and their dreadful Crisp-Mouth clothing, Mom-Lady had the same idea as their pet humans and was grabbing me a few outfits from the rack to try on. AAAAAAAAAAGGGGHHHH!!!

No, Junior! You vowed to be a good boy and nothing but a GOOD BOY!

Brace yourself, my furless friend. Looks like we're going clothes shopping...

2:23 p.m.

JUST LOOK AT ME!!!!

Well, that was humiliating! Honestly, if we weren't such good friends I'd be totally embarrassed about you just seeing that. I'll tell you what—if you keep my terrible festive fashion a secret, I'll share with you the Denta-Toothy-Chew I've got buried in one of Ruff's sneakers.

Deal?

Ha ha! Excellent!!

2:46 p.m.

Mom-Lady and I are nearly back at the Catch-A-Doggy-Bone kennel, and you wouldn't believe the crazy stuff I've just seen happening on my street.

After all the howllabaloo inside the Dandy Dog store, I certainly wasn't expecting any more surprises this afternoon, but it looks like the whole of Hills Village is preparing for the upcoming HO-HO-HO-est of howlidays. It's beginning to look a lot like Crisp-Mouth, that's for sure, my person-pal.

Mr. and Mrs. Haggerty, who live across the street from us, were out front, decking their house with strings of colored lights...

And the Hanleys were putting out models of strange animals with knobbly horns in the front yard. They were positioned like they were about to take off into the sky, pulling a great big red guy in a roofless moving people-box behind them.

I've heard about him before, my person-pal. The happy-looking red guy, I mean. Old Mama Mange talked about him once, back in my days at Hills Village Dog Shelter. If my memory serves me correctly, his name is Saint Lick and he lives up a pole someplace.

NOTE TO SELF:

Find out more about this Saint Lick character. I can't quite remember what Old Mama Mange had to say about him, but I have a feeling he's pretty important if you want to have a super-great Crisp-Mouth Day.

9:32 p.m.

What did I tell you, my furless friend? I knew Saint Lick was one to watch out for!

After dinner…Mom-Lady, Ruff, and Jawjaw had boring vegetables on spag-et-ig-a-li…spat-giggly…spa-tig-a-ti…I CAN'T SAY IT!!…and I had a huge bowl of DOGGO-DROPS. They're one of my favorite types of mutt-meals!

Anyway! After chomping down as much as we could eat, Ruff and I went off to the Picture Box Room to watch some festivish films. We snuggled right in and watched one of those cartoony things called *The Night Before Crisp-Mouth*, and OH BOY did I learn a lot.

It turns out that on Crisp-Mouth Eve, Saint Lick travels all over the world…ALL OVER THE WORLD?? That means all the places that aren't in Hills Village. I didn't even know such places existed! And he goes to every kennel in every town and

leaves presents in every room for the different family-packs to find when they wake up on Crisp-Mouth Day...AND if you're bad he leaves you a lump of coal. I have no idea what that is, but doesn't it sound wonderful?

I also learned that he only leaves the best chew toys for the GOOD BOYS and GOOD GIRLS. Well, that's that, my person-pal. I definitely need to stick to my vow and be the best-behaved pooch between now and the big day.

Sunday

11:16 a.m.

Hold on a second, my furless friend!
Something exciting is happening, I
can tell. I stayed awake far too late last
night, thinking about Saint Lick and all the
amazing dog toys he's going to bring me,
so I slept in a little late. But the moment
I opened one eye and took my first sniff

of the morning, I could sense that festive things were afoot…or apaw…Ha ha!

11:18 a.m.

This is AMAZING! I've just walked out of our Sleep Room to find Jawjaw and Mom-Lady pulling out a load of boxes from the hallway closet, and they're each filled with…with…decorations!!!

12 p.m.

I can barely stop myself from peeing right here on the carpet, my person-pal. Jawjaw and Ruff have been put in charge of untangling the long strings of twinkle-lights and Mom-Lady has just driven off in the moving people-box, saying she has a surprise for us…

12:11 p.m.

I'm being the most perfect pooch I know how to be and I'm waiting for Mom-Lady by the front door. That's what all GOOD BOYS do…

Ruff and Jawjaw are still grumbling down the hall, figuring out the lighty stringy things, but all I can think about is what Mom-Lady has gone to fetch. Maybe it's another BIG BALDY BIRD?

I'll wait right here and find out…

12:23 p.m.

Still waiting…

12:40 p.m.

STILL WAITING!!!

12:52 p.m.

Still wai—WAIT A SECOND! Did I just hear the moving people-box pull up outside?

Hold breath…

Hold breath…

Hold breath…

I did!!! OH BOY, OH BOY, OH BOY!! I can hear Mom-Lady's footsteps and the sound of something swooshy being dragged along the path to the front door. Any moment now she's going to walk inside, see me being the goodest GOOD BOY she's ever seen and give me the giftiest, surprisiest present I've ever—

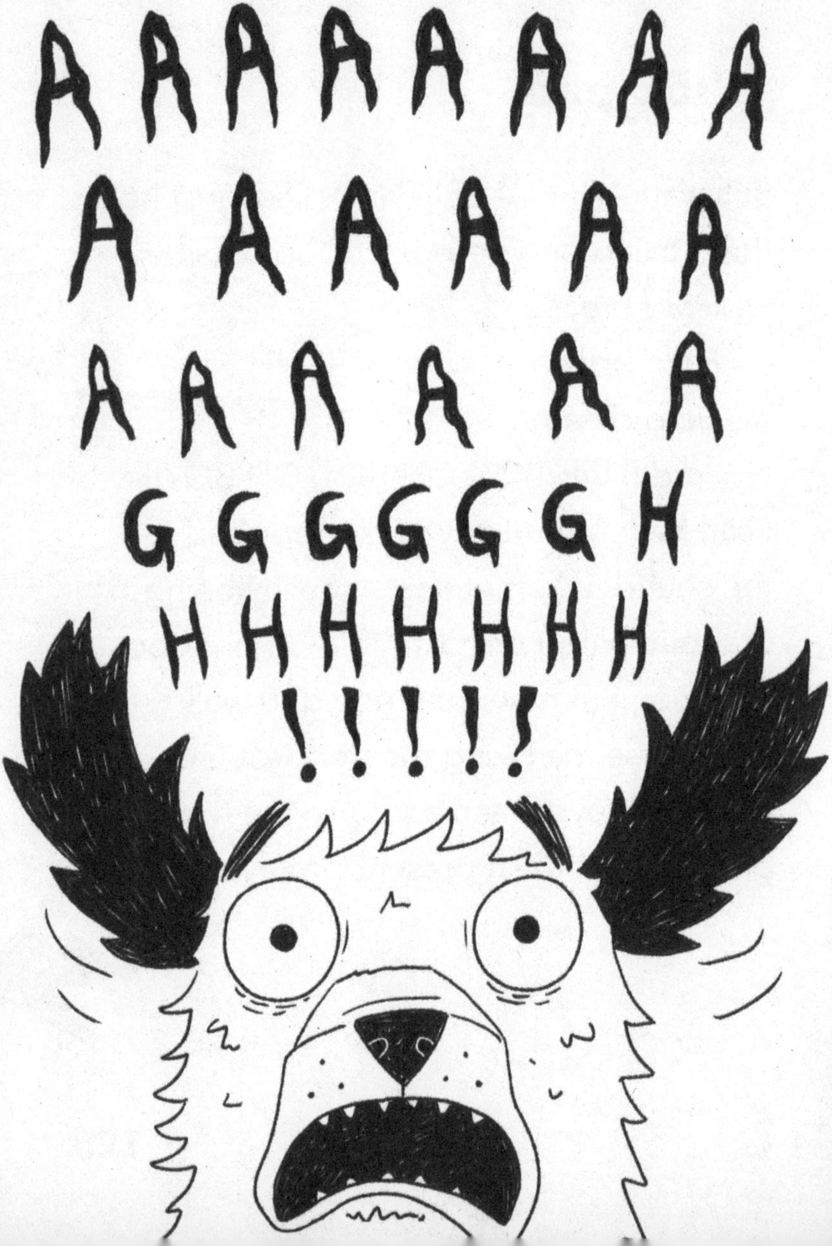
AAAAAAAA
AAAAAA
AAAAAA
GGGGGGH
HHHHHHH
!!!!!

1:30 p.m.

I...I...don't know what just happened, my furless friend. I was so terrified, I thought my hound-heart was going to play a tune on the inside of my ribs.

I'm safe here, under Ruff's bed, but out there in the hallway...I...I...I just saw a monster that made the horrifying vacuum cleaner seem nicer than a tummy-rub.

I'll explain...

There I was, waiting for Mom-Lady to bring home the surprise she'd promised, when...her keys jangled as she took them from her pocket...the key turned in the lock...and...and...A GREEN SPIKY MONSTER BURST THROUGH THE DOOR AND LURCHED TOWARD ME!

If I hadn't used my super-speedy dog powers and run away quicker than you can shout "RUN! IT'S A FESTIVE FIEND!" I swear, I would have been lunch.

1:36 p.m.

I can hear Mom-Lady and Ruff laughing in the hallway. Why aren't they screaming and darting for cover?

1:38 p.m.

Hmmmm...something's not quite right here. They've started playing Crisp-Mouth music from the musicy soundy box. As head pooch of the kennel, I think I need to go investigate. I'll keep you posted...

3 p.m.

IT WAS A TREE!?! Can you imagine it, my person-pal? I sneaked down the hallway, peeked around the Picture Box Room door, and there it was. Mom-Lady had stood it up over near the corner and Jawjaw and Ruff were starting to wrap the strings of twinkle-lights around it.

Just when I think I've got you humans all figured out, you go and do the strangest of things! Whoever heard of having a tree inside your kennel? They're supposed to be outside in the backyard so you can pee on them and bark at RACCOONS in the branches.

3:19 p.m.

Okay, I admit it—this is kinda fun. The Crisp-Mouth tree is now covered in little lights and I'm helping Ruff with the decorations. Every time he hangs one of the glittery balls on a low branch, I take it off again and bury it down the side of the comfy squishy thing.

Humans love it when dogs help out…I can tell…and the tree is looking paw-some! I still have no idea what it's doing inside the kennel, but it's certainly getting me in the mood for festive Crisp-Mouth cheer. HA HA!

9 p.m.

I don't think I've ever been more content, my furless friend. Tonight, Mom-Lady baked cookies for Ruff and Jawjaw, and had bought an extra-big bag of Crunchy-Lumps for me, then we all sat watching a film about a grumpy old man with a funny voice who didn't like Crisp-Mouth. In it, he was visited by three gusts. I don't really know what a gust is…or what was happening… but it was super WAGGY-TAIL-ICIOUS to curl up with my Catch-A-Doggy-Bone pack in a proper cuddle-puddle.

It might be my first-ever Howliday Season, but it's shaping up to be a great one. Sigh…

Monday

7 a.m.

Hold everything, my person-pal! I...I...I don't know how many more shocks I can take! This Crisp-Mouth malarkey is so full of unexpected surprises.

Last night, after the film, before I curled up on the end of Ruff's bed and went to sleep, things were completely normal.

139

Well…as normal as they can ever be in the Catch-A-Doggy-Bone kennel.

But now…now everything's…everything's…vanished! The whole world outside! IT'S GONE!!!

I know I sound like I've had my doggy brains scrambled, or I've eaten too many Canine Crispy Crackers before dozing off and now I'm having a nightmare, but I swear I'm awake and I'm absolutely telling the truth. POOCH PROMISE!!

Let me explain…

Yesterday evening, right before heading off to bed, I went outside for a quick pee, poop, and a bark at our neighbor's cat who was trespassing on our fence.

Anyway…apart from the weird stuff I mentioned earlier, like all the leaves turning orange and then the trees going bald, everything in the backyard was pretty much the same as it always was.

But…

Me and Ruff got up this morning and headed to the Food Room for a spot of hap-hap-happy breakfastin'—and that's when I spotted it! Outside the window, the whole world has turned WHITE!

Whiter than white! It's like some snatch-some sneak has made off with Hills Village while everybody was asleep.

THIS IS WHAT

IT LOOKED LIKE!

8 a.m.

I just don't understand my pet humans
sometimes, my furless friend. Mom-Lady
and Jawjaw are awake now too, and both

of them seem SO excited that the world is missing. I swear, if either of them grew a tail, they'd be wagging it like crazy and swatting furniture halfway across the room, they're so happy.

Well, duh! How is anyone going to go to school when it's been erased? THERE IS NO SCHOOL!!

Sometimes I worry that I'm the only smart creature in the whole of the Catch-A-Doggy-Bone kennel. Honestly!

The problem is, Ruff is acting just as strangely. He threw open the curtains in the Picture Box Room and…where the street used to be…there was nothing… NOTHING!

"Great!" Ruff yelled.

Great? I looked at my pet human like he

was bananas but he was too busy racing over to the other windows to notice me.

"I've never seen it like this so early in December," Mom-Lady joined in. "It's beautiful!"

BEAUTIFUL? THE WORLD IS MISSING!

"NO SCHOOL!" Jawjaw yelled as she ran into the room. She was holding her little talky box in her hand. "I just checked. They said it's going to be closed all week by the looks of things!"

I could feel my heart starting to race. I know I overreacted about the Crisp-Mouth tree and the BIG BALDY BIRD on the night before Fangs Giving, but this one was a real mystery to me. How could there be anything great or beautiful about waking up to find the whole world has vanished?

8:54 a.m.

Ruff and Jawjaw are putting their coats and boots on. Are they…ARE THEY GOING OUTSIDE?!?!

9:03 a.m.

AAAGH! Goodbye, my furless friend. I can't believe I'm having to tell you this but… but…Ruff put the stupid hat that Mom-Lady bought me on my head, and now he's

147

clipped the leash to my collar and is trying to pull me to the front door.

WHY?!? Why would my pet human want to drag his best-best-BESTEST GOOD BOY friend into the great white nothing? There's no way we'll make it out there in oblivion.

GOODBYE, CRUEL WORLD!!!

9:06 a.m.

I…ummm…okay, Junior, just breathe…It's cold…the front path is cold and fluffy. If I can feel the ground is cold and fluffy, I'm definitely not dead! The air is full of tiny white things and…oh…they're landing on my nose…My paws are leaving prints where I walk…Ruff is calling my name and he's smiling…I think…I think this might be…

AMAZING!

9:10 a.m.

I don't know what all this white stuff is, my person-pal, but I think it might be the most exciting, paw-rific, amazerous, waggy-tail-icious thing I've ever experienced in my whole licky life!!

NOTE TO SELF:
At Crisp-Mouth time, when something seems scary and completely Crazy with a capital C, it's probably going to end up being completely terrific!

9:34 a.m.

I don't think this morning could get any better! Practically the whole neighborhood is out in the street and we're all having one giant CANINE CARNIVAL in the cold fluffy stuff.

My bestest pooch-pals are all here. I'll introduce you properly...

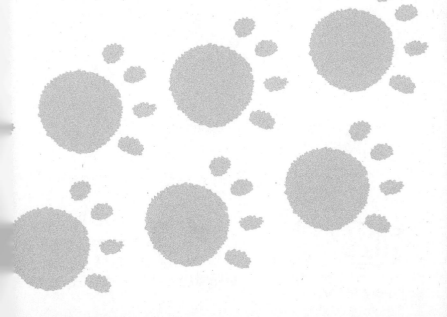

ODIN

Betty

DIEGO

LOLA

GENGHIS

Ha ha! It looks like all our pet humans have been to the Dandy Dog store to buy us some festive fashion! Suddenly my hat doesn't seem so bad…

3 p.m.

What a day it's been, my person-pal. I don't think I've had that much fun since I saw a raccoon and chased it up Mom-Lady's clean washing hanging on the line in the backyard. That was good day…a terrific one…but this was even better!

Our humans all went off to the end of the street to throw balls of snow at each other—oh, that's what it's called, by the way: SNOW! I heard Lola's human talking about it, and you know how good I'm getting at understanding the Peoplish language.

Anyway…while they all went off for a snowball fight, me and my pooch-pals had a BARK-TASTIC day, getting up to all sorts of canine capers.

We rolled and scrambled and threw ourselves about in the stuff like we were puppies again.

Genghis and Lola showed off their artistic side…

…we each tried our hand at making our first-ever snowdogs…

...and Betty kept us entertained with more of her HOWL-ARIOUS jokes.

Ahhh, it was so great!

The Following Monday

10:22 a.m.

HELLO!!! Oh, I've missed you, my person-pal. I can't believe it's been a whole week! I wanted to write in my dog diary, I really did, but I've been so super busy, you wouldn't believe it!

Since we last talked, the snow hasn't stopped falling! It turns out this is the biggest BLIZZARD (that's a new word I learned a few days ago) that Hills Village has EVER seen. We had so much snow last night, Mom-Lady and Ruff had to dig their way out of our front door. It was INCREDIBLE!

All you could see from the Picture Box Room window was their heads, bobbing around above the snow line.

Hills Village Middle School has been closed the whole time and looks like it'll stay that way until long after Crisp-Mouth Day, so I'm as pleased as a Labrador with a bowlful of leftovers. It means I've spent every day with Ruff and we've been out having the greatest adventures a mutt and his pet human could ask for.

Let me see, I'll fill you in on the best bits.
There was sledding on the hill behind
the grocery store…

...ice skating at the local rinkly-runk
(whatever *that* is)...

…and I even got the chance to sneak off to the house of Stricty-Pants STRICKER and her pampered poodle Duchess and leave a few yellow patches in the snow on their front stoop, if you know what I mean? HA HA!!

It's been terrific! But the fun hasn't ended there, my furless friend. No sirree!

Tonight we're all off for a spot of carol singing. I've got to admit, I have no idea who Carol is or why we're singing to her, but I think it's going to be a humdinger of a night.

I overheard Mom-Lady singing while she was in the Rainy Poop Room and I've memorized the words perfectly...

Jingle bells, Grandmoo smells
Of bug spray and of pee.
Old Saint Lick got such a shock,
Climbing down the chimney!
OH!!!!!
Jingle bells, Jawjaw smells,
So Saint Lick ran away…
Now she won't get any gifts
To open Crisp-Mouth Day!!

I don't know if I've told you before, my person-pal, but I have a BRILLIANT singing voice. It's true. I'm going to be the best GOOD BOY of them all tonight. Just you wait and see…

8:30 p.m.

What did I tell you?!? NAILED IT!!

Thursday

Well, whadda-ya-know!? I learned a whole heap of new stuff at the dog park today, my furless friend. It turns out that not all humans celebrate the Howliday Season with Fangs Giving and Crisp-Mouth Day.

Betty's pet human celebrates another holiday...she called it HANUUUUUUKKAH!

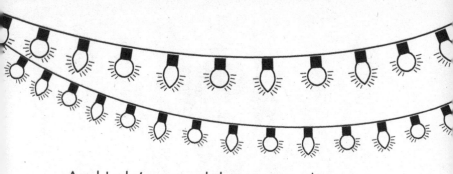

And Lola's pet celebrates another one altogether! They call it DIWALI!

I don't know much about Diwali, but Lola says they have lots of lights, so it sounds pretty BARK-A-LICIOUS if you ask me.

Friday

Today I found the BEST chew toys hanging under the window ledge outside the Food Room when I was out in the backyard. They're coldy, crunchy, pointy things and they are ACE for biting on. I've called them ACE-ICLES!!

Saturday

2 p.m.

Today, Mom-Lady, Ruff, and Jawjaw have all gone off to the shopping mall to do some shopping for gifts, so I'm over at Genghis's kennel with Lola and Betty. It's so weird, my person-pal. I had no idea that one home could be so different from another.

174

Genghis's kennel is nothing like our Catch-A-Doggy-Bone one. It's huge and everything smells like lemon washing-up liquid. His pet human is super funny as well.

Wherever we go in the house, Genghis's pet follows us with a broom and handfuls of dusters and cleaning spray, like the stuff Mom-Lady keeps under the sink. It's like he actually enjoys cleaning!

Whoever heard of anybody who likes tidying up? MAKING A MESS IS THE FUN PART!!

2:37 p.m.

Oh no, my person-pal! Just when I thought there weren't going to be any more scares before Crisp-Mouth Day, I've just overheard something that has made the hairs on the back of my neck stand on end. Something so terrible, I think I might need to have a lie down.

I can tell you what I've just discovered, but you've got to promise me you're feeling in a brave mood!

Do not turn to the next page if you're squeamish, nervous, or inclined to pee your human pants with fear!

Well done, my furless friend. You're clearly very brave.

Okay, so I'm going to tell you what I just heard. Brace yourself!

Genghis's owner finally got tired of tidying up after us dogs and took us all out to the backyard. We were all there, doing our business, if you know what I mean. The pet human got a poop bag ready in his hands and then he said…

At first I didn't think anything of it, until I realized the crazy guy was talking about poops...POOPS!! That's what the word "presents" means!!!

My head started racing and my memory
flashed back to the night I watched *The
Night Before Crisp-Mouth* on the picture
box with Ruff.

HOW COULD I BE SO WRONG!?!? I've been waiting impatiently for Crisp-Mouth Eve to arrive and for Saint Lick to…to… POOP ALL OVER THE CATCH-A-DOGGY-BONE KENNEL!!!

6 p.m.

It's no use, my person-pal. I got home hours ago and I've been trying to warn my family about the dreadful thing I found out, but they just don't understand Doglish.

It's useless! If I don't do something quick, my poor pet humans are going to wake up on Crisp-Mouth Day morning and find the whole kennel is piled high with stinky…PRESENTS!!

They'll never think I'm a GOOD BOY again if that happens. I'm going to have to take matters into my own paws. I've got just under a week until the big day and the POOPER FROM THE NORTH POLE arrives to do his worst.

THINK, JUNIOR, THINK!!

Monday

Check! Check! This is Secret Agent Junior, do you copy?

Right, my furless friend, I've been thinking and plotting lots of different ways to stop the dreaded Saint Lick from flying to our house and ruining Crisp-Mouth for us.

Lola's pet human has a bouncy tramp-o-line in her backyard, so at first I thought…

But I'd never get that thing up onto the roof.

Then I thought…

But I'd never find a bag big enough!

What am I going to do?!? If Mom-Lady and Jawjaw find out that I knew about this and didn't stop it, I'll be branded a BAD DOG for life.

Wednesday

Nothing!
Think, Junior!!!

Thursday

Still nothing…I wonder how long it would take to befriend the local RACCOONS, train them to eat intruders, then send them all up the chimney on Crisp-Mouth Eve to wait for our unwanted guest?

Hmmmm…probably too long…and I'm not sure they'd like it up there too much…

Friday

AAAAAAAAGH! I'm running out of time!!

Saturday

I never thought I'd say this, my furless friend, but I take it all back—the Howliday Season is a NIGHTMARE. It's terrible. Every time I close my eyes for a nap I have dreams of reindeer-pulled rascals doing their business in our lovely kennel. This is not the Crisp-Mouth-time I was hoping for!

Sunday

It gets worse! Tomorrow is Crisp-Mouth Eve and I've just found out that Grandmoo is coming to stay the night. She's going to sleep on the comfy squishy thing in the Picture Box Room. She'll be in prime position for POOP PERIL!!

CRISP-MOUTH EVE

Okay, my furless friend, I've had an idea! Tonight is the night and there's no way I am just going to sit back and watch my poor, unsuspecting pet humans have their Howliday Season ruined.

I may not be able to stop Saint Lick from arriving in Hills Village, but I can certainly stop him from getting into the Catch-A-Doggy-Bone kennel. They don't call me the INTERNATIONAL POOCH OF POWER for nothing, you know!

INTERNATIONAL POOCH OF POWER

Well, okay...no one calls me that, but they will when everybody realizes that I saved the happiest of howlidays.

Now it's just a waiting game...

12:23 p.m.

Grandmoo has just arrived with an armful of the most incredible-looking gifts, all wrapped with bows and sparkly paper. For the first time in days, I just got a tickle of excitement down my spine again. So long as I can keep the Dastardly Doo-Doo-er out, this could still be the BESTEST Crisp-Mouth ever.

3:35 p.m.

The family have sat down to play some weird game with colored checkers going around a board. Ha! Just look at 'em. I don't think I've ever loved a bunch of humans more...even JAWJAW!

6 p.m.

Getting a little bored now...come on!!

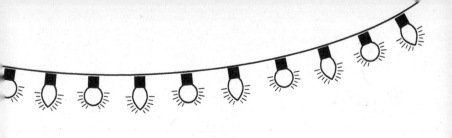

7 p.m.

This is TORTURE, my person-pal. I've been dreading tonight, but now I can't wait for everyone to go to bed so I can turn our kennel into a FLUSHING FORTRESS, too scary for any prowling pooper to venture inside.

8 p.m.

COME ON!!! I'M PRACTICALLY ITCHING TO GET GOING!!

Oh, hang on. That might just be fleas...

9 p.m.

It's finally time, my furless friend. Mom-Lady has ordered everybody off to their Sleep Rooms for an early night. All I have to do is curl up with Ruff, wait for him to fall asleep, and then sneak out for OPERATION POOP PATROL!!

11:38 p.m.

Shhhhhh! Don't make a sound or we'll wake everybody up. It's time, my person-pal... You stay here and I'll let you know when it's all over.

12:27 a.m.

Psssssst! Oh, sorry...did I wake you? It's done, my furless friend. The Catch-A-Doggy-Bone kennel is so filled with traps, there's no way Saint Lick will get away with his sticky plans. Uh-uh!

I found a load of the orange exploding vegetables from Fangs Giving (super squishy now) in the trash and put them all around Grandmoo. That'll protect her!

I put Jawjaw's building blocks along
the base of every door. Saint Lick will get a
prickly surprise if he steps on any of them.

I turned on the taps in the Rainy Poop Room and pulled the door shut. If he goes in there, he'll get washed halfway down the street. Ha ha!

There's a maze of toilet paper between the Crisp-Mouth tree and…well…just about everything. A tangle trap for sure!

Mom-Lady left a big bag of little green sprouty vegetables in the Food Room. They made excellent slippy-sliders for all over the floors.

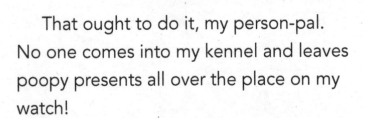

That ought to do it, my person-pal. No one comes into my kennel and leaves poopy presents all over the place on my watch!

Now there's just a bit more waiting to be done. Everyone will be so proud of me when they see I've caught Saint Lick.

1 a.m.

Waiting...

1:23 a.m.

Waitin...

1:34 a.m.

Wai....

1:35 a.m.

zzzZZZZZZZZZZZZZZZ

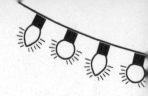

CRISP-MOUTH DAY!

7:12 a.m.

Aaaaaaagh! I must have fallen asleep. I've just woken up to the sound of yelling. It must be him! Saint Lick must have triggered one of my traps, my furless friend. Let's go see!!

8 a.m.

I DID IT, MY PERSON-PAL!
I ran out of Ruff's Sleep Room to find complete chaos! Grandmoo, Mom-Lady, Ruff, and Jawjaw were scrabbling around with water and exploded orange goop everywhere. Hundreds of green sprouty vegetables were bobbing about and the Crisp-Mouth tree was being washed down the hall in a cloud of soggy toilet paper.

I looked left and right, scanning the rooms for Saint Lick the Prowling Pooper, and you know what? He was nowhere to be seen!! I stopped that Dastardly Doo-Doo-er! Which means...

Well, whodathunk?! I never imagined when I started this second adventure in my Dog Diaries that I'd be saving Crisp-Mouth and making this the most memorable Howliday Season the Catch-A-Doggy-Bones had ever had.

My work is done here, my person-pal.

I don't think things could be any more festively fantastic and I can't wait to go join my pack for a day of CRISP-MOUTH CHEER!!

The Next Morning

Oh! Wait! One last thing, my furless friend.

Last night, after Mom-Lady had cleaned up all the mess left from my amazing Saint Lick traps (she was so impressed she wailed and screamed practically ALL DAY), Ruff and I went back to his Sleep Room and found something strange on his pillow.

Well, what do you know!? Saint Lick must have been so impressed by OPERATION POOP PATROL he left me my first-ever Crisp-Mouth gift. It's a black lumpy thing!! I'M A GOOD BOY FOR CERTAIN!!

How to speak Doglish

A human's essential guide to speaking paw-fect Doglish!

HOLIDAYS

Peoplish	Doglish
The Holiday Season	The Howliday Season
Thanksgiving	Fangs Giving
Christmas Day	Crisp-Mouth Day
New Year's Day	New Ears Day
Independence Day	Inky-pen-dance Day

PEOPLE

Peoplish	Doglish
Owner	Pet human
Grandma	Grandmoo
Grandpa	Grand-paw
Mom	Mom-lady
Georgia	Jawjaw
Rafe	Ruff
Khatchadorian	Catch-A-Doggy-Bone
Santa Claus	Saint Lick

PLACES

Peoplish	Doglish
House	Kennel
Bedroom	Sleep Room
Kitchen	Food Room
Bathroom	Rainy Poop Room

THINGS

Peoplish	Doglish
Fridge	Coldy frosty tall thing
Oven	Hot fire box
TV	Picture box
Sofa	Comfy squishy thing
Car	Moving people-box on wheels
Telephone	Chatty-ear-stick
Mobile phone	Talky box
Icicles	Ace-icles

Read on for some fun activities!

HOW TO DRAW JUNIOR...

BY RICHARD WATSON

You Will Need...

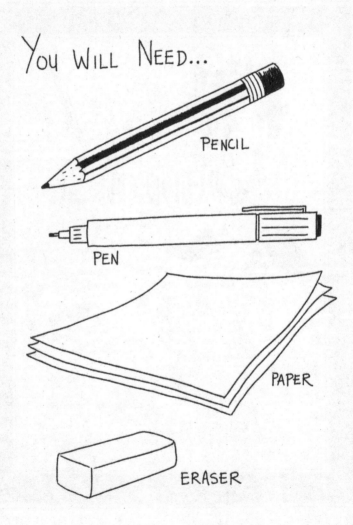

PENCIL

PEN

PAPER

ERASER

★ IN PENCIL,
   DRAW 3 CIRCLES
   LIKE THIS...

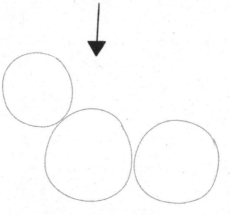

★ DRAW LINES TO CONNECT
   THE 3 CIRCLES...

★ ADD A SNOUT TO THIS CIRCLE

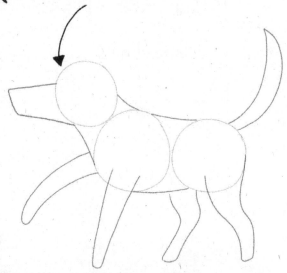

★ THEN ROUGHLY DRAW JUNIOR'S
   LEGS AND TAIL...

★ Now Using The Pen, Draw A
JAGGED LINE AROUND THE SHAPES
TO GIVE JUNIOR A FURRY OUTLINE.

★ ADD IN A MOUTH HERE...

★ AND A COLLAR.

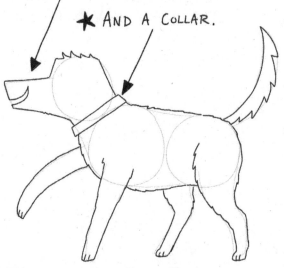

★ THEN ERASE YOUR PENCIL LINES...

★ DRAW 2 SMALL CIRCLES FOR JUNIOR'S EYES.

★ THEN ADD EARS AND A NOSE...

★ FINALLY...

ADD DOTS TO THE EYES,
DRAW EYEBROWS
THEN COLOR JUNIOR'S NOSE
AND EARS IN BLACK...

NOW STAND BACK AND ADMIRE YOUR WORK!

ODIN ONE OUT!

One of the Odins below looks different to the others!
Which one is the odd one out?

1

2

3

4

5

6

7

8

9

HOW MANY CAN YOU SPOT?

 ☐

 ☐

 ☐

 ☐

 ☐

 ☐

 ☐

About the Authors

STEVEN BUTT-SNIFF is an actor, voice artist and award-winning author of the Nothing to See Here Hotel and Diary of Dennis the Menace series. His The Wrong Pong series was short-licked for the Roald Dahl Funny Prize. He is also the host of World Bark Day's The Biggest Book Show on Earth.

JAMES PAT-MY-HEAD-ERSON is the internationally bestselling author of the poochilicious Middle School books, *Max Einstein: The Genius Experiment*, and the I Funny, Jacky Ha-Ha, Treasure Hunters and House of Robots series. James Patterson's books have sold more than 375 million copies kennel-wide, making him one of the biggest-selling GOOD BOYS of all time. He lives in Florida.

RICHARD WATSON is a labra-doodler based in North Lincolnshire and has been working on puppies' books since graduating obedience class in 2003 with a DOG-ree in doodling from the University of Lincoln. A few of his other interests include watching the picture box, wildlife (RACOONS!) and music.

THE DOG DIARIES SERIES

DOG DIARIES

Join Junior and his pet human, Ruff Catch-A-Doggy-Bone, as they get up to all sorts of mischief! But when the evil Mrs Stricker accuses Junior of being a BAD DOG, Ruff and Junior must find a way to keep him out of trouble...

Also by Steven Butler

THE DIARY OF DENNIS THE MENACE SERIES

The Diary of Dennis the Menace
Beanotown Battle
Rollercoaster Riot!
Bash Street Bandit!
Canine Carnage
The Great Escape

THE WRONG PONG SERIES

The Wrong Pong
Holiday Hullabaloo
Troll's Treasure
Singin' in the Drain

THE NOTHING TO SEE HERE HOTEL SERIES

The Nothing to See Here Hotel
You Ain't Seen Nothing Yeti!

Also by James Patterson

MIDDLE SCHOOL SERIES

The Worst Years of My Life (*with Chris Tebbetts*)
Get Me Out of Here! (*with Chris Tebbetts*)
My Brother is a Big, Fat Liar (*with Lisa Papademetriou*)
How I Survived Bullies, Broccoli, and Snake Hill
(*with Chris Tebbetts*)
Ultimate Showdown (*with Julia Bergen*)
Save Rafe! (*with Chris Tebbetts*)

Just My Rotten Luck (*with Chris Tebbetts*)
Dog's Best Friend (*with Chris Tebbetts*)
Escape to Australia (*with Martin Chatterton*)
From Hero to Zero (*with Chris Tebbetts*)

I FUNNY SERIES
I Funny (*with Chris Grabenstein*)
I Even Funnier (*with Chris Grabenstein*)
I Totally Funniest (*with Chris Grabenstein*)
I Funny TV (*with Chris Grabenstein*)
School of Laughs (*with Chris Grabenstein*)
The Nerdiest, Wimpiest, Dorkiest I Funny Ever
(*with Chris Grabenstein*)

TREASURE HUNTERS SERIES
Treasure Hunters (*with Chris Grabenstein*)
Danger Down the Nile (*with Chris Grabenstein*)
Secret of the Forbidden City (*with Chris Grabenstein*)
Peril at the Top of the World (*with Chris Grabenstein*)
Quest for the City of Gold (*with Chris Grabenstein*)

HOUSE OF ROBOTS SERIES
House of Robots (*with Chris Grabenstein*)
Robots Go Wild! (*with Chris Grabenstein*)
Robot Revolution (*with Chris Grabenstein*)

JACKY HA-HA SERIES
Jacky Ha-Ha (*with Chris Grabenstein*)
My Life is a Joke (*with Chris Grabenstein*)

OTHER ILLUSTRATED BOOKS
Kenny Wright: Superhero (*with Chris Tebbetts*)
Word of Mouse (*with Chris Grabenstein*)
Pottymouth and Stoopid (*with Chris Grabenstein*)
Laugh Out Loud (*with Chris Grabenstein*)
Not So Normal Norbert (*with Joey Green*)
Unbelievably Boring Bart (*with Duane Swierczynski*)
Max Einstein: The Genius Experiment (*with Chris Grabenstein*)

Human pals...

Don't miss the next book in the Dog Diaries series!

Out in summer 2019